G000140330

Reverence Library
Volume One

A Sing Statistics book

SING STATISTICS

Published by Sing Statistics, Edinburgh

Copyright © 2011 Sing Statistics

Individual copyright to the works published in this volume
are held by the respective authors. No part of this book may
be reproduced, stored in a retrieval system, or transmitted
by any means, electronic, mechanical, or otherwise, without
prior permission of the authors and publisher.

Printed by Oddi, Iceland

Designed by Jez Burrows
Set in Plantin and Aperçu

ISBN: 978-0-9569295-0-1

First Edition
Limited run of 1,000

Reverence Library
Volume One

Galleons
Nikola Tesla
The Trans-Siberian Railway

A Sing Statistics book

A note from the editors

Reverence Library is a series of abridged pocket encyclopaedias inspired by fact and reworked by fiction. They are intended to complement more *conventional* reference books—vast, unwieldy things that they are—which remain stubbornly devoted to the former, downright suspicious of the latter, and far from pocket-sized. Sing Statistics do not recommend citing material from *Reverence Library* in any formal texts, unless you have prior experience before academic or journalistic tribunals.

Table of contents

Galleons

The Spire of Ice

Joshua Allen

∎

People in my line of work hesitate to use the word *cursed* because it implies there are forces beyond our control, and control is the whole reason we got into this business. But when it comes to *The Spire of Ice*, we just kind of shrug and call it like it is, because listen:

She was a Manila galleon, originally called *El Tiburón del Oro*, built in the Philippines to run spices and porcelain and silk and whatnot to Acapulco, where the goods were then dragged across Mexico to Veracruz and shipped off to Spain. And she was *big*. A thousand tons, four masts, thirty cannons firing nine-pounders that I have personally seen turn a man into crimson smoke.

But: There was a mutiny on board *El Tiburón* in the first twenty minutes of its maiden voyage. Before it even got out of the *harbour*.

Some mutinies are carefully orchestrated, mapped out to the smallest detail. Most are the result of someone who's had enough of the bad food and bad rape—but that takes at least a couple days at sea. In this case it was the powder monkey, couldn't't've been more than twelve years old, who took issue with the captain strangling his mother to death in a whorehouse a few days earlier.

The captain was running through his usual announcements—"do not address me by name, do not look into my eye with

your eye, do not enter my chambers after sundown, or ever"—
when the powder monkey vaulted down from the foremast,
pinned the captain to the deck, and shoved a handful of lit
smokecherries (handmade from sugar, gunpowder, and finely
ground *conium maculatum*) down his throat. In the ship's log,
the captain's last words were reported to be "an horrific gargle
that shall stay with us to the grave and beyond."

Once the smoke cleared, the crew gathered around the
bloated, stinking body to chastise the powder monkey:

"Why'd you do that, lad?"

"He kilt my mum dead," the powder monkey cried. "Choked
her lifeless!"

"Kilt a dozen other whores at the Velvet Glove, what of it?
Some men have peculiar needs!"

"I myself have to wear a lady's frock and be struck with the
Bible in order to know pleasure!"

"'Tis not your place to cast judgment, or your little balls
of death-smoke!"

"And now we have no captain, and his knowledge of the sea
was second only to his love of strangulating women!"

"I am the captain now!" the powder monkey said, his voice
shrill and unbroken.

And yes, the Law said that the Captain-killer became the
Captain. But these things usually played out with a second
party stepping in to kill the Captain-killer, and then maybe a
few more stabbings or eye-gougings, and then we finally get to
a point where all that's left is some undisciplined psychopath
and a collection of even-keeled types who just want to do their
job, get paid and go home. This arrangement is actually pretty
ideal for your average transport ship, but *El Tiburón* was not
so lucky. The crew just shrugged and let the powder monkey

run things and a couple hours later they were tangled up in *el cenagal*: a peaceful, shallow stretch of water where, years earlier, a ship had mysteriously sunk. And then snagged a second ship. And then a third and fourth and tenth and twentieth until the whole region was nothing but a rickety deathtrap of shattered masts and rotting sails. *El cenagal* had thus become a popular spot for buccaneers to sit and wait for booty to get caught in the web. Within a day of *El Tiburón*'s entrapment, they had leisurely murdered the entire crew, pilfering its fresh supply of goods and bullion and weaponry, and then sailed off, feeling oddly unsatisfied.

Years passed. Then, one fine April, a wealthy landowner named Marikit Abayari launched an ambitious project to dredge up the ships caught in *el cenagal* and refurbish them to build his own private fleet. His scouting ship got caught in an eddy and capsized, killing all aboard.

Decades tumbled into centuries, and then a second, more successful, effort was made by Eleanor Jickett (of the Rhode Island Jicketts, restless with slave wealth) to resuscitate *El Tiburón*. Using state-of-the-art crane technology, she dredged up the galleon, badly battered but still basically brand new, and had it towed back to shore. It was then torn apart and sent, in hundreds of crates, to Newfoundland—the starting point of her exploration of the Arctic. There, *El Tiburón* was rebuilt into a luxury research facility, complete with ten cabins, a chest-high orrery, a darkroom for the photographers, and a prow reinforced with iron.

Eleanor rechristened the ship *The Spire of Ice*, the name coming from her recurring nightmare about a spiky iceberg looming in the distance, jabbing heavenward, indistinct, never getting any closer but forever threatening, a Thing that would someday destroy her, not a matter of *if* but *when*.

When turned out to be a few days after the *Spire* set sail. A rare parasite (a stowaway in the rum) got into the crew's intestines and dispensed with its hosts in—to quote Jickett family biographer D. R. Bernhardt—"a literal explosion of such terrible biologickal horror that I cannot bring myself to describe it here out of respect to my readers and Our Lord."

The *Spire* floated adrift for months in the frigid North Atlantic, deck strewn with perfectly preserved innards, until it meandered close enough to fishing waters to be discovered by a posse of Kalaallit, whose prophecy stated that said a ghost ship would one day come to carry them off to their version of Heaven, a land carved from frozen akvavit where promiscuous ice maidens swam just below the surface of the water, their tender parts clean and insatiable.

The Kalaallit cheered, packed their things, and let the winds take them. Before long they were lost, their coastal fishing techniques useless, and they were forced to feed upon the refrigerated remains of Team Jickett. And of course they suffered the same explosive, parasite-fueled end.

When scavengers eventually stumbled upon the bloody wreckage, the sight inspired one crewmember to write a collection of terrible poetry called *There Must Certainly Be No God*. It featured poems entitled: "O Chiaroscuro of Gore," "That Which Was Never Meant to Be Witness'd," and "A Man's Soul is Bloody and Foul-Smelling."

The scavengers managed to keep from eating the tainted meat and instead opted to haul the poisoned ship to the nearest port of call and cut their losses. The *Spire* was then purchased by "philanthropist" James Diamond of New York City, New York, who had it hosed down and rebuilt as a *pleasure barge*, decked out in gaslights and orchids and silk. She escorted high-paying customers out into international waters where they could enjoy the company of expert courtesans in a wide range of themed cabins: The Samurai Suite, The Sherwood Forest Encounter, The Igloo Room, Ye Olde Operating Theatre, &c.

It is in this capacity that I got to know the *Spire* firsthand, taking a number of enjoyable cruises on ill-gotten lucre, succumbing to the blandishments of one Miss Emerald Skye of The French Revolution Room and her skillful handling of the so-called *love guillotine*. It was also in this capacity that I experienced a particularly virulent strain of gonorrhea, and I was not alone—hundreds of customers suffered the same fate. The sterling reputation of the *Spire* was ruined and James Diamond found himself in debtor's prison.

Miss Emerald Skye, who'd been socking away most of her earnings, found herself suddenly able to afford the galleon, her home for twelve of her twenty-two years. She bought it in cash and sold off the paraphernalia (camisoles, chemises, corsets, fine hosiery, things of frill, leg cuffs, cats o' nine tails, feathered domino masks) to re-hire the crew. I offered my services as, say, a purser, but she took me by the hand, gingerly, and said she was going to a place that had no need for me. And no need for mutinies or whores or hemlock or viruses or ice.

I asked her where this place was. Did it have an address? Perhaps I could write her from time to time? She said: *No letters will reach where I am headed, and nothing you do will ever earn you admittance.*

And thus the *Spire* sailed off, finally shedding its curse, leaving it squarely on my shoulders.

fig. 1

fig. 2

Replacements
Paul Ford

▮

There was a situation with the galleons six months ago and now, finally, we are having the meeting. Mona, James, Othar, Ku, and I. James starts talking in acronyms, SKUs and PRNs. Ku rolls his eyes at that.

At James's insistence we watch focus-group footage of people looking at pictures of galleons. "It's basically a boat," says one woman in an orange blouse. "I don't like the hull?" says a nervous-looking man who brought his dog. "Too big," said a third man, clubfooted.

I liked the texture of this industry. Checking things off with a quill pen at port. Warehouses filled with casks. The smell of oiled wood, the sight of a room filled with cannonballs. The vile things that sailors said, or ate. There was a pet seal at the docks that wore a sweater.

James leans back in his leather chair, watching the focus group, shaking his head. Of all of us he has the most to lose. His wife is sick and he has six children; his older brother's gambling debts have devoured his father's fortune. If he loses his position he could end up living in Boston.

Ku scowls.

How can this be happening? Why am I here? My childhood was all pictures of fat boats with beaks and mizzenmasts. I made my father buy woodcuts of sea-scenes. He hung them over my bed with nails and string. His father was a fisherman so he had no interest in boats. After I married I kept novels about sailing in our bedroom and would read them while my wife, rest in peace, read the Bible.

Why wasn't I at sea? When I was 14 I wanted to go, desperately, but I was worried about my knots. Instead I apprenticed as a scrivener at the shipping agency, later moving up to accts. When I was 19 I married my second cousin. There was no reason not to go to sea besides fear.

When my wife was ill I held her hand and wept. I was feeding her mushed apples. You were always a coward, she said, and then she vomited a sweet-smelling bile over her lace bib and expired. I have thought of that moment many times since.

I boarded a galleon only once, two years ago, after ten years in the industry (staying on land had become a sort of superstition). But the entire staff was expected, with wives (of course I had none by then); not to go would have seemed peculiar, especially as the event was held on a Wednesday; I would have been the only person in the office. I walked up the gangplank, flushed when I arrived on deck. It was happening to someone else. How could I be here, adrift at sea?

There were boat tours offered by the sailors, most of whom, I noticed, were missing teeth; obviously they wanted to get a closer look at the wives, and steal a pinch or two in the shadowy holds. I elected not to go along; I had no wish to interfere and a concern that in the darkness I might also be pinched. Of course from my cutaway diagrams I already knew exactly what I'd find below decks..

At sunset, after a day of sun and treats and punch, we sailed beneath the larger of the two city bridges into the near port. I'd never seen the underside of the bridge before. I could see the bolts that held it together, each the size of my hand. A dozen other boats of equal or greater size were in the harbour.

On cue a golden vessel appeared in the distance. A figure in white stood at the bow. This was a visiting queen in a dress covered in pearls. She was the reason for our departure. On the quartermaster's notice sailors shot off all of the cannons. It was deafening. My hearing only returned in stages. I could hear the river lapping against the hull before I could hear the voices around me. And then I heard the gulls, and, behind me sailors muttering the vilest words about the visiting dignitary. Had I been a gentleman I would have cautioned them. Children were fishing off the riverbanks.

It should have been obvious then that there was little room left in the world for our kind of boat. But in the company of the wind and the cannon-smoke and the gleaming royal in the distance I was nearly overcome; I leaned against the railings and closed my eyes, enraptured. I felt like anything but a coward.

The focus group is winding down. On the video the man's dog is scratching itself. The screen goes blank. The country of the visiting queen, I have read, is recently overcome by Turks.

Well, says James, that was that. These people.

We have a warehouse with casks of wine, said Othar. We have solid, proven leadership.

Mona puts her long hands over a folder. Sighs, and looks down the table to me. We are looking at possibilities, she said. There is coal. There are wagon-wheels. Sloops. Tin. We are not without options. There is, she continues, an ocean slickness off of Norway.

She looks to me. Am I interested? She wants to know.

Am I interested? I am interested in galleons. But do I write Mona's name in the margins of my night-reading, over and over? Perhaps I do. I say I am interested. Like James I have no wish to end up in Boston.

Mona tells me that the slickness is six thousand feet on a side and who knows how many fathoms deep. It may just be a slickness. But what if it's more? We should get on top of it. We have to stop thinking in galleons. I have thought in galleons for my entire life. Ku is looking out the window. James is tapping his pen on a pad of paper, slowly, rhythmically.

I will go out into the ocean on some modern sloop. I will wear oilskin. I will be lowered in a rowboat and I will dip a cup in the muck. Perhaps I will put a finger in and taste it. Perhaps a beast will swim up from the depths, some creature with huge white eyes, and swallow the boat, and me, up.

I think it could be the best thing that ever happened to us, said Mona.

That's the sort of thing that people say that when they have a terrible illness.

It's good work, she says. This is the new world.

Meaning not galleons.

traversed *the world* in search of

GREAT TREASURES

...t when the need arose... I was ready to do battle.

and I was always victorious.

An undignified end perhaps..

y contemporaries, ey festered.

Or were dismembered and re-used..

at on and forgotten..

But on clear nights, people say they see my ghost on the horizon..

ey don't.

But it's a nice thought.

Pages is Waves

Michael Crowe

▌

At the time of writing Ell is swimming around the ocean collecting driftwood. Hammered together en route, she's building a galleon, which, once completed, will be sailed quietly home. Splashlessly backstroking, she pictures the completed ship safely docked, her bedcovers warmly pulled over.

So far it's half built: multi-decked, long beaked, mizzenmasted, sink-sailing. Ell's keen to include a fourth mast, a bonaventure mizzen, however, problems are multiplying:

Years at sea: Fatigue.
Cold: Water.
Food: Sparse.
Sharks: Hi.
Nails: One left.
Hammer: Dropped.

Nevertheless, hearty whistling work continues. The ideal find is oak, but anything bobbing by is brill. Shoes and weird wicker form much of the hull. Plastic bags are sewed and saved for sails. Lassoing a gigantic styrofoam turkey, Ell wonders:

What is the largest unknown sea creature?
How close is the nearest one?

How many million splinters make the average galleon?
Is this a southerly wind?
How many miles have I walked in my dreams?
How does my street taste, bouncing around in one huge mouthful?
Does Delanie miss me?
Why am I doing this?

A teenage storm passes. Blobs of salty sunshine. A single cloud, shaped like a tap, hovers above Ell. Out of the spout: rain.

At the time of reading the deck is mostly made. Sixty metres of chirpy invention. Enthusiastic branches and barrels slide back n' forth, exactly as you imagine it. There are no cannons, no cannon balls, just Ell, waving. While you read the next sentence, she winks at the moon. Glowing, she thinks of choreographing a moonlit dance for the deck which takes into account the shove and pull of a storm. She considers the cannon balls, fired in a panic years ago, at the bottom of the ocean. A low, crouching constellation. A wet dot to dot pic.

Past the time of writing, Ell is back home. The galleon is docked. Ell is surrounded by microphones and questions. Nodding and shaking and nod-shaking her head, she thinks of her bedroom, in which every object is gently breathing. The books, the table, a mug, another mug, a model galleon, the stapler, pencils, perfume, posters, all delicately inhaling and exhaling, soft, out of sync. The rise and fall of the sea is quite like a breathing chest.

THE CAPTAIN

THE SOLDIER

THE SAILOR

THE DOCTOR

THE SAIL MAKER

THE CARPENTER

THE MONK

THE STOWAWAY

THE HORSE

BACK STAFF

HIS WIFE'S PORTRAIT

ON

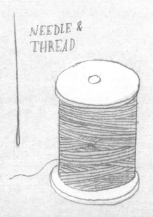
NEEDLE & THREAD

T.E.
HENRI
GRACE A DIEU

Nikola Tesla

Birds

Matthew Allard

∎

The man rolled over to face the winter light. It was late day, sunset, and outside the unwashed windowpane a hint of orange almost made the sky look warm. The crystals along the base of the glass, however, served as a frozen reminder of New York City in January, cracked and bone white. Inside the front bedroom of Room 3327 it was stuffy and cramped and a meticulously clean sort of messy: a discarded jacket, a cane, a stack of thick texts. Papers were littered about in precise piles. There was another room laid off to the side, cloaked in darkness and disuse.

On his side, the man felt gravity pulling his organs down, gravity stitching his skin and bones to the mattress. His eyes blinked, his pupils took in the hard light. It flashed harshly, out and out, out and in.

Something wasn't right.

The pigeon stood on a tattered chair beside the window. At first, it appeared only as a bundle of stockings. Then, as the speckled light waxed and waned, the bird took shape: a stout beak, mottled monochrome feathers, coarse feet, reptilian eyes.

"We do believe," the pigeon began, "that it is good to see you again."

The man shielded his eyes. The pigeon cocked its head before hopping to the floor in a quick forward motion. It tiptoed toward the man.

"I haven't seen you." The man's voice was low, hushed and sandy. The words seemed to break apart at his lips.

The bird was across the room, and then instantly upon the ragged quilt that covered the lower half of the man's body. Its claws bit into the loose threads and its head bobbed back and forth like a harbored boat. The man still rested on his side. Moments passed and the darkness in the room increased. The bird did not fade.

"You were gone," he said, finally, not looking at the pigeon.

"Of course, friend. We come and go as we please, same as always." The voice was almost non-existent. It seemed to come not from the bird but from the room itself.

"I had hoped you'd come back. Visit me again, that's all."

"After everything you've done?" The pigeon extended a wing dramatically. "We'd not miss the opportunity to say goodbye."

The man's eyebrows, just wisps, reacted to the word. *Goodbye.* Like a listless doll he rolled onto his back, returned to the position he had been sleeping in since that afternoon. He was sleeping so much lately. The pigeon ruffled as the mass beneath it reoriented. The man could see the bird better now, though it was harder to breathe in this position. It perched on his chest, above his heart, glowing white in the swimming grayscale of the room.

After a deflated pause, the sinking of the news, the man sighed, "This is goodbye."

It started as a child in Smiljan, part of what was then the Austrian Empire. He was a boy who wore his idiosyncrasies like a superhero's cape. He recited books from memory, suffered unexplainable hallucinations and held protracted chats with a beloved housecat. When he was first spotted whispering amongst the birds it seemed all the same, expected: "Clearly the boy is not right," strangers might mutter under their breath; "What next!" they wondered. He never explained the conversations, though. Even when asked. Ultimately, the situation was received as just another bizarre—yet harmless— development for the very peculiar child.

When he became a man he displayed more extra-terrestrial behaviors. The number three became vitally important; he avoided all contact with dirt; and he shunned women, even as the most beautiful came calling. Of course by then he'd enrolled in university and proven that his mind was not only uniquely eccentric but also quite brilliant. His quirks and the continued obsession with birds could be overlooked still. For the strange boy who'd rapidly become a curious man was not mentally handicapped; he was just *different*. Though he led a life so veritably misunderstood, he was proving that somewhere inside his vast brain, there was remarkable genius to behold.

He became an inventor.

"We've brought you a present," the bird said.

The man's chest felt pressurized, as if thousands of gallons of water were pressing in on it. He was sweating and, for the first time in his life, uneasy with their conversation.

"I do not think I can—"

"Hush." The pigeon shook as if laughing. "Does a mind as bright as yours not appreciate any and all knowledge?"

"Of course, yes," the man said too quickly.

"We thought so. You will not build us this. The vision is but only a gift…"

In the inky gloom of the hotel room, the man tried to steady his breathing. He blinked once. He blinked again. He focused his gaze on the alien pearls of the pigeon's eyes. This is how it always happened. This is where he saw the parts. This is where the pieces, the very jigsaw-like particles of science, were shown to him.

When the man returned to his body, uncertain how much time had passed, it was still dark outside.

"Of course the foundations of such a mechanism have already been set in motion," the bird waxed in a modern philosophical tone. "Give us another 15 years and someone shall build it. We're getting there decade by decade." It fluttered to a perch upon a bed knob and revealed: "They'll call it the laser."

The man paused. Then, "Light Amplification by Stimulated Emission of Radiation. The laser."

"Precisely, friend. Bravo!"

"An invention for the future... Brilliant!"

"It's quite something, yes."

"No, no. It's amazing!"

The bird released a disembodied laugh, "It is certainly not our best." Slowly, eerily, its beak crept into an impossible smile. The look, the implausibility of it, made the man instantly queasy. His pulse quickened. "Can you keep a secret?" The bird's words came from nowhere. They were whispered yet they echoed throughout the room. "There's something more we're...dying to share with you."

The chilling delivery slithered over the man's bare arms. He shivered and felt the pressure in his chest increase. There was that sensation again, the feeling of something out of place, not right. The man lay there, motionless and unanswering, aware of the bird's twisted smile and sinister, unblinking eyes. In his right ear, so close that he could feel its hot breath, he heard something hiss: "A farewell secret."

The bird took flight like a nightmarish crow. Its shadow darker than the dark, it circled the air just above him. It circled—and the man's heart skipped. That pressure!

When the second vision completed, the man returned to his body while morning light snarled against the window, intense as a spark. How had so much time passed? The man felt excruciating white blindness. There was a horrible wailing, too, and he was vaguely aware that he was causing it.

"Have we struck you with lightning?"

The bird perched on the chair beside the window, nonplussed. It had built a nest with a blanket stripped from the bed.

The man stopped wailing, but the images, like ghastly photographs, were quite seared into his mind. He could still see the parts operating in bold synchronicity, repeating their haunting ballet. It would use technology he'd created earlier in life, and it would use it in a way he'd never intended.

The new vision had physically hurt, and this time the usual excitement the revelations brought was replaced by a gleaming horror. The man on his deathbed knew what the invention would be used for. He could see it all from the inside out.

"That one should not be built!" With jagged movements he worked himself to a seated position: "That one should *not* be built, you hear?"

"All these years we've shared our designs with you. We thank you. By your talent they were forged into physical, tangible possibilities. But do not forget the knowledge has always been ours."

"But you must not share those plans with anyone else!"

The bird cocked its head dangerously to the left. If possible, its prehistoric eyes clouded over black. "You will not decide." The bird's voice had been like wind, faint. But now the man could clearly feel the words. The syllables slapped into his face: "No one lives forever. You are too old. You are too tired. Someone else will carry on our work."

"You can't find someone else! You can't!" he spat, choking on the sound. "I made inventions for good. For the advancement—"

"—This is *our* advancement."

The roaring force of the words knocked the man from the bed to the floor where he wasn't strong enough to lift himself. He trembled there, barely breathing, his chest tight as a fist. He'd made a terrible mistake. And as his vision began to fade, each breath harder to take, the pigeon cooed and came to his side. And as he took his last breath, the bird shuffled its feathers. And as he left, it was there alone, a stupid winged thing pecking for stray crumbs between the cracks in the floorboards.

Rachel is 16

Daniel Beirne

▌

Nikola Tesla was standing shirtless and sipping tea. He spotted a single grey hair in his moustache and bent it with the tip of his tongue. He trimmed it with a pair of small scissors and dressed silently while looking out of the window. The sun was setting at a mere 4:42 on a grey Manhattan in December. In the cold of the coat room, he took a pair of fur-lined gloves off a shelf, for the first time this year, they would not leave his pocket until April. He started the two-hour journey to the country.

Rachel Westinghouse was digging a miniature grave in the hard earth behind the manor in the country. "Rachel, come get dressed!" her mother yelled from inside. Rachel placed a small mouse, caught in a trap near dawn that morning, in the tiny grave she had dug with a serving spoon. The little mouse's features had been splayed by the impact of the trap, and the cool dirt was a welcome calm to the violence of its appearance. "Rachel! Now!" Rachel filled in the dirt, wiped the spoon on her dress and flew into the house and up the stairs, pushing the curls of her hair from her face.

"This day is not about you, my dear," Rachel's mother, her thin and strong arms yanking a brush through Rachel's hair, spoke with a smile. "Your father only has a Christmas celebration once a year, and I do not think it much to ask of you to put your busy schedule on hold for one simple evening." A taught and stinging ponytail, this level of tightness was reserved for special occasions. Rachel believed it to be a way of ensuring she would constantly be smiling, voluntarily or otherwise. "Mother, don't help me dress, I'm not a baby." She stood waiting by the bed, holding still with her party dress in hand, refusing to move until her mother grabbed her sewing ball of pins, a candle, and left. Once the door clicked closed and her mother's footfalls reached the stairs, Rachel threw the dress down on the bed and rushed over to her writing desk:

> I heard a snap in the night and got up to check and it was a mouse. Father laid traps in the dining room because he was acting mad and screaming when he saw a mouse during Sunday dinner last. He yelled all about the party and his employees and how we would not be embarrassed as a family so he laid some traps. If you asked me, I would say his behaviour over the mouse was far more embarrassing than any actual mouse could be. My father is funny and strange and often surprisingly dim, for a man who has accomplished so much. I think maybe I will make him a character in a story one day. A mad simpleton who eats too much buttered beans and fish.

Nikola Tesla arrived late from the city as the snow was falling thinly in the still night. He had expected to be late, but not to miss dinner, he now feared silently to himself that he would not eat until Sunday. He trod carefully up to the house in his leather shoes, not built for the country snow. "Tesla!" said Westinghouse, as he answered the front door, the warmth of the party behind him, "Come in!" Tesla entered humbly amidst the chatter of the guests, and shook a few hands of those he knew from the labs. "I want to introduce you to my family!" yelled Westinghouse, he yelled most often when he was excited, and Tesla had excited him at many points this past year. "This is my wife Marguerite, and our daughter Rachel. She's a genius, Tesla, like you!" Tesla smiled and looked around, "Oh yes?" Rachel looked down and away, her ponytail only allowing certain positions of her head to be of any comfort. "Yes!" shouted Westinghouse, as if challenged, "Only sixteen years old and already she's written a novel! An entire novel, Tesla!" Tesla looked at Rachel, trying to catch her eye, saying to the three of them, "Oh yes?" Rachel said nothing in reply, her cheeks reddening. "It's about a race of moon men," said Westinghouse, handing Tesla a small glass of port wine, "they speak only in numbers, if you can believe it." Tesla felt a small swell in his heart, his face flush, perhaps still adjusting to the warmth of the house. "That sounds fascinating," he said, and moved on to the rest of the party guests.

Rachel watched him from her place near the door to the kitchen, as he moved through different conversations, for no less than a half an hour. He talked with his hands, sometimes greatly impassioned, other times subtly placing the word in the air, about lightning and energy and the world as a system. She knew with a blushing certainty that she was in love. She felt the soles of her feet become damp in their stockings, she felt a nervous kind of tremor in her breath as if her lungs were slightly shivering, and she felt suddenly beautiful. She thrust out her chin and postured her head at an angle as if to say, to no one in particular, *I have arrived.*

After the smoking began, Westinghouse and some of the guests moved to the billiard room to enjoy brandy and cigars, and Tesla went out on the back porch to watch the snow falling. He hummed an old tune that his parents used to sing. Rachel came quietly out to the porch holding a roll of bread, sliced with a bit of ham and mint. "Mr. Tesla?" she said, looking for someone who might hear her but there was no one else. "Rachel." "I've brought you a bit of food, I noticed you haven't eaten all evening, and you missed dinner, I just thought you might be hungry." She handed him the sandwich. "Thank you, Rachel. I am hungry." He looked back at the snow, and Rachel began pulling at the pins in her hair. Tesla carefully picked out the ham as casually as he could and ate the mint and bread. Rachel let her hair down and shook it free in the cold air. They looked at each other. "I buried a mouse out there this afternoon." "I see. Tell me about your story. Your novel." She put her hands to the buttons on her dress.

Westinghouse and the guests spoke about the French Revolution and the so-called "Industrial Era". "I think a train is a train is a train, if you ask me," said one of the guests, "it's not a sign from God." "I wonder how all this will affect people," said another. "How it will affect people? How do you feel? That's how it affects people!" shouted Westinghouse. He missed his shot and laughed.

"Are they men or women, these moon people?" said Tesla, and Rachel looked out at the snow, a question she had never thought to ask. She had used all her focus and energy to talk about the story, and now she was dizzy in a spell of excited humiliation. Of course he would ask such a question, he loved her as much as she did him. "Or maybe do they have no gender at all?" asked Tesla, his breath like the steam off a kettle. "Yes, they have no gender. They are just people," she replied, the sweat on her feet growing cold and her shivering lungs near quaking with emotion. "Fascinating," said Tesla, as he took the fur-lined gloves from his pocket, he looked at her shivering. "My dear, let's go inside, you're cold." "No no, I want to stay out here," she said, trying at once to stiffen and relax, anything to stop the shivering, anything to stay exactly where she stood. "At least take my coat." "No no, thank you." "Take my gloves," he said and put the gloves on her. They fit loosely on her tiny hands and as he put them on, she brought them to his thin face and kissed him dumbly on the mouth. "I love you," she said, a curl of hair between her eyes. Tesla looked down and away, suddenly staring at the ham he had tossed in the snow. His kettle breath steady and calm.

As Westinghouse said goodbye to a pair of guests, Tesla came up behind with his coat on. "Tesla! You're leaving!" Westinghouse and his wife sent him with a bit of bread and some apples, a lovely warm couple, and Tesla did not look back as the tails of his coat billowed behind him and he left into the night. Rachel ran up the stairs crying, a large pair of leather gloves on her hands. She sobbed into her room and closed the door and headed straight for the candle at her writing desk:

I am in love with a man that I hate. As long as I live I swear to almighty God I will never utter the most hateful words in all the language to anyone I ever meet in my life: "silly little girl".

Tesla came into his apartment, through the cold coat room and started a small fire in the stove near his small bed. The dregs of his tea, now near freezing, remained in the cup and he sipped at it. He undressed and eased his delicate body under the cold sheets of his bed, and thought for the first time that he occupied very little space on this Earth.

Nikola Tesla Was Not Sorry
Meaghan O'Connell

■

Better he might have fared, poor wight,
Hadst thou not given him a gleam of heavenly light;
Reason, he names it, and doth so
Use it, than brutes more brutish still to grow.
With deference to your grace, he seems to me
Like any long-legged grasshopper to be,
Which ever flies, and flying springs,
And in the grass its ancient ditty sings.
Would he but always in the grass repose!
In every heap of dung he thrusts his nose.
Goethe, *Faust*

Nikola Tesla was walking through the park much like you and I would on a beautiful day with little to do. Nikola Tesla was off to the market and turned a corner, maybe, because he had the time. Nikola Tesla was 24 years old and learning again to turn corners when he felt like turning corners, the way we know to do when we are young but must relearn. Nikola Tesla was 24 but not the way we think of it. He knew all the words to Goethe, knew all the words to lots of things, and counted his footsteps in threes while he said the words out loud. Said the world out loud. The ground trembled beneath him, but only in his head; at this point it trembled only in his head.

His heart hurt all the time and the sun hit him like a train to Budapest. It hit him like never sleeping, like reading books through the night, like working through the day for things, for ideas, but never knowing what you'll be able to do about them. The sun hit him and hurt him, hurt his eyes and his brain and his heart, hurt him like knowing the things we needed from him were somewhere hidden but could not find their way out. The sun hurt him like needing to draw something very important out from somewhere you would rather not go.

The sun was setting and Nikola Tesla walked with his friend in their dress pants with their sleeves rolled up, squinting into the sky or that's how I imagine it, kicking rocks around in the dirt in Croatia, absent-mindedly reciting poetry back when you could still do things like that. Back when nights without sleep amounted to something, whether your mother cried for you or not. Whether or not your father sat at your bed when you had a breakdown and told you that he would send you to engineering school against his will because he saw in your eyes that you had to go.

Nikola Tesla kicked rocks around the pathway with his hands in his pockets. He counted his heartbeats. The sun sunk down over the trees and the milk awaited him at the marketplace, unbought. He kept saying words in German out loud in front of his friend the way we don't do anymore,

> The glow retreats, done in the day of toil;
> It yonder hastes, new fields of life exploring;
> Ah, that no wing can lift me from the soil,
> Upon its track to follow, follow soaring!

He stopped. He whirled around. He moved the world around.

He drew the thing in the back of his head, pulled it right out, right past the poetry and the sunset, past the dress pants and the rolled-up sleeves; he drew it with a stick that was lying by the feet of the friend who was scratching his head and wondering if Nikola Tesla had forgotten the rest of the words to *Faust*, Part 1, and hoping he would not start up again. He drew it over the milk and the eggs and the butter and over 24 years of headaches and language and no sleep. He drew it whole, drew it complete. The sun waited to see what became of it. His heart beat too quick for counting. He did not finish the poem. He ran.

Nikola Tesla ran home, past the sun, past the market, past the woods and his friend. He moved swiftly around corners and would soon tear through the kitchen empty-handed. He would try not to look his mother in the eye, try not to see her arms folded sadly over her nightgown while his own hung long and thin at his sides, while his hands moved quickly at edges of his pockets as he stood silent before her—fingertips tapping out a song in notes of three: ring finger, middle finger, pointer; pointer, middle, ring. He would stop but then get moving again, hoping she would not see that he forgot the butter and that he forgot the eggs and he had done nothing but let her down his whole life. He would try not to hear her little voice when she yelled "Nikolaaa!" up the stairs just to punish him. He had not made it to the market today, did not get them honey for the tea, did not bring back wood for cooking with, did not know how to love them, did not know how to tell them that he didn't, but the motors in his head still shifted so he looked away from the throat-clearing mother and the newspaper-fluffing father opposite her at the table—a poet and a priest each, both after him, both threatening him in one way or another. He drew the picture in the sand over and over in his mind, over the sounds of his consciousness singing, cheering. They wanted things to be different and him to be better rested; he drew the picture. They wanted to carve him into good health and scholarship. He drew the picture in the sand again and again and watched it work, rejoicing. They only wanted, like all parents must, to not be worried by the frailty of him, to instead see more than his eyes alight beneath that dark hair, that dark, Serbian hair, always parted down the middle with an equanimity that made the rest of him jealous. They had mourned the loss of him since childhood. They had always wanted things he couldn't do.

But the motor in his head was still moving, and he could only be so sorry, only had so much room in himself for it, counting his heartbeat and all of the stones in threes on the walkway up to the front door, his face all lit up like that.

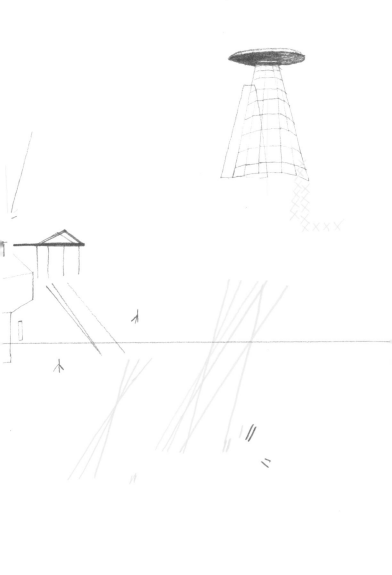

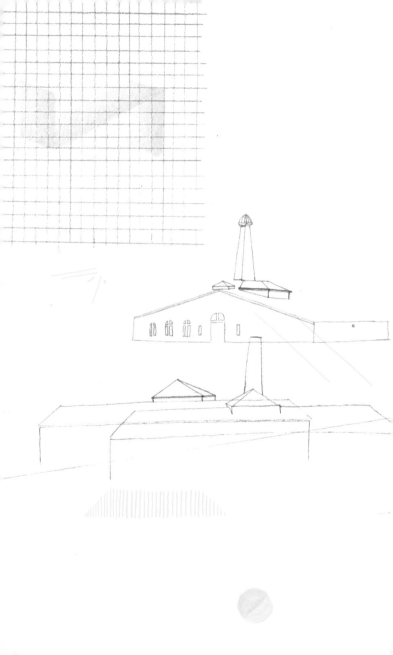

The
Trans-Siberian
Railway

Tsar Nicholas II Rides The Trans-Siberian Railway
John Moe

▉

The Trans-Siberian Railway. Dig that name! Majestic! Linger on those vowels! A regal name, befitting a Tsar, no? And I have my own train on it. The Tsar's Train. I am happy to be here. Some big shots might get their own train car, sure, but I get A TRAIN. Why? Tsar. Tsar!

And I ride it across my nation in total majesty. We roll through all these cities. Tyumen, Krasnoyarsk, Ulan-Ude. I mean, who ever thinks of these places? Seriously, I go months at a time without Ulan-Ude crossing my mind. Call me a snob if you want but why would I? It's not like I see it on TV or hear it on the radio, those things haven't been invented yet. What are they going to do, e-mail me? Come on. It's pre-Soviet Russia. Shut up.

And then there's Taishet! Do you know why we even have Taishet? To serve the Trans-Siberian Railroad. That's it. That's why they exist. So when you're in the Tsar's Train like I am, well, imagine how that must feel. Special train, rolling through a city that exists to serve a railroad that my grandfather schemed up, my father guided toward reality. Chugga chugga toot toot y'all, here I am, Nicky the 2, riding in style.

But that's not why I love the Tsar's Train. I love the TT because of the gaps between the cities. Those long stretches of land and nothingness. Of grass.

You wouldn't believe how much grass you see when you take the train all the way through Siberia. Wild grass, left to its own devices. And it's not like trees where they can grow thick or tall or mossy or something cool when left alone. Grass just sits there, grows a little, dies off, grows again, dies, maybe gets fucking eaten by some fucking animal or something. I don't know, I'm not a zookeeper (I'm a Tsar). But then you watch the grass go by for HOURS and HOURS (because what are you going to do, watch a DVD?) and even though you know it's a completely stupid form of life, at least it's living, it's carrying out its simple little process that it was put on earth to do.

And what am I, The Tsar, doing? Nothing! Watching it. And look, it's not just grass that I feel this way about. The Trans-Siberian Railroad takes you through mountains and by lakes and through variable amounts of snow, depending on the season. Goddamn nature just doing all the goddamn budding and blooming and decaying and whatever, and here I sit doing none of it. Now, this kind of realization can really freak a fellow out. I may command great armies but I don't photosynthesize, I have no real natural function. I'm a freak by comparison, an unholy monster. IT NEARLY MAKES ME INSANE.

So nature continues in its smelly stupid way outside, away from me, and I'm on this railroad that God never intended to exist. But the Tsar's Train is beautiful. I can smoke my cigars, I can read. I can drink. It's opulent on the ol' TT. Fancy curtains, big poofy chairs. It's so grotesquely luxurious that I can rise above nature and embrace the alienation and feel like a god myself. Or at least an amazing rock star. Like Axl Rose during Appetite For Destruction. And what's really great, and I can't stress the importance of this enough, is that it's all built around being really comfy for ME! Nick the Deuce!

Here on the TT, life makes way more sense than it does in the rest of the world. For one thing, I wasn't supposed to be running Russia this early. My father got sick, then sicker, then dead, all way early. I was in charge from age 36. 36 is late for grad school, far too early to be Tsar. Then at my official coronation was the Khodynka Tragedy. Have you heard about this? Khodynka Field in Moscow. Word gets around that any peasant showing up to celebrate will get presents. Presents! Like I think it was a bread roll, a sausage, a mug, and some gingerbread. Now I've said this before but THERE WAS NO PLAN TO GIVE OUT PRESENTS. I mean, I'm bearded but I'm not Santa Claus, right? Still, some 500,000 people show up anyway looking for these things because they think the new guy just happens to have half a million mugs ready to hand out. Then the cops show up (okay, my cops) and everyone panics and 1,389 people are trampled to death. Which is a really nice way of saying, "Hi Nicholas, welcome to world leadership. Some idiots wanted gingerbread and now they're dead and it's all your fault." It was a terrible time for me. For those people and their families too, I guess, but mostly for me because I'm the Tsar and I matter more. Not boasting, just fact.

But again, even when I was dealing with all that, I kept thinking about the Tsar's Train, the place where all other concerns go away and I am awash in opulence. Because I built this railroad, pretty much. I was the one who appointed the ministers who oversaw the building process and it was me at the ceremony to formally kick off the construction. A ceremony, I might add, WHERE NO ONE DIED. At least that I know of.

Railroads, man. And I'm all about connectivity. Have I told you about my big journey around the world? The Eastern Journey? Well, now is a perfect time then since we're in this train car and all that there is to look at outside is GRASS for DAYS. And I'm the Tsar so you have to listen to me or I'll have you killed. Kidding. Lighten the fuck up.

See, it's kind of this bullshit thing that all the tsars have to do when they're young, a sort of educational jaunt around the world so that when we get back to Russia, we can act like we know what we're talking about. So in October of 1890, I set out on this trip, going through Greece, Bombay, Singapore, Japan, all the way back around to the eastern side, the ass end, of Russia. From there, I traveled over land and on the rivers as far as Orenburg where I could catch a train back home to St. Petersburg in August of '91.

Now, it's important to note a couple of things: uno, this was not like some crazy Europe trip after you graduate college where you and your buddy Moondog backpack around and stay in hostels and drink beer and try to score with German chicks. This was me with an entourage of diplomats attending state functions. Par-dee, right? Wrong. Secondly, that last part of the trip where I traveled across Russia (which is big) was done without the Trans-Siberian Railroad.

And you know what that meant.

Grass.

But if I had just had this train. If I had just had the TT. If I could have traveled back home in style on the railroad I single handedly built with the appointment of those guys I appointed, that would have been incredible. That would have made the whole thing work. Imagine me, a young Nick Squared, having learned the world, then traveling across the country that would be mine, largest country on the planet mind you, in a train built for me. A hero. Would have given me context and, frankly, some much-needed self-esteem.

Train wasn't built by then, though. Train would be built later. And you know what? Here's the sucky part. I never got to travel the full length of the Trans Siberian Railroad (or Railway, Wikipedia says either one works) in the Tsar's Train. Could never eat that plum. So, yeah, okay, I was being a little dishonest with you here. You're not really getting a letter from THE TSAR aboard the TSAR'S TRAIN! Sorry, fatty. Shoot me.

Because frankly by the time the dang line was completed, I had some other pressing concerns.

Like the pogroms in which thousands of Jews died. Or my ultimately disastrous decision to get Russia involved in World War I. Whew, that was quite a move. I mean, if you made the argument that that one decision led to the Bolshevik Revolution, the rise of the Soviet Union, the Cold War, and a global population going to bed at night convinced that they would eventually be obliterated by nuclear weapons, well, I could not argue with you. A lot of shit went down is what I'm saying.

The TT on the TSR. I think about it a lot lately. How the vehicle of perfect transcendence and that long ride through the grass—bet I would have come around on the grass—was within my reach but not my grasp. Could have been so great.

They could have let me take one ride on when all the weird shit was going down. The railroad finally opened in 1916, they could have let me take one last long ride in my special train to see the grass and sit and think for days. And then they could have shot me in Vladivostok. Instead, I'm here in stupid ass Yekaterinburg in the stupid ass Urals, getting shot along with my wife, my children, three loyal servants, and my doctor and who knows why he stuck around for that.

That's my story. Sorry Trans-Siberian Railway. Would have been cool. Peace. N2.

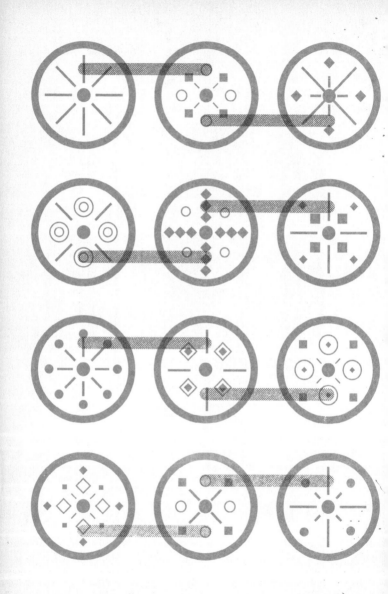

Bylina
Tess Lynch

∎

My mother Jane is eleven, and she is in Leningrad. It is 1958, and she has just stepped out of the Tovstonogov Bolshoi Drama theatre. It is ten at night. The sky is bright, pale blue; the clouds are unmoving, smoky scarves. She stands in the square, behind her parents and three siblings. She feels someone tug at the sleeve of her summer coat, and turns around to see a girl a few years older than she is. The girl wears a scarf over her hair.

"Rich?" The girl asks. Jane shrugs. "Rich? Is cost much money?"

"You'd have to ask my mom," replies Jane. The girl looks at my grandmother's back. My grandmother is wearing fur. The girl smiles at my mother.

"Rich," she says, still smiling. Her teeth have silver caps on them. She touches Jane's lapel, and walks away, rubbing her fingers together.

Jane's father John reads *Soviet Life* when they are at home, in a suburb outside of Boston. He settles into an old armchair when it arrives by mail, lights a cigarette, and drinks a highball of rye whiskey while he reads. When Jane passes by the doorway on her way to the kitchen, he nods at her without looking up and mumbles his nickname for her, which is "brownhead." At dinner he will be silent until, finally, clearing his throat:

"Nice steak, Mom," and my grandmother would say thank you, and he would get up, pleased, and retire to the den, where he would worry and pat the dog on the head and think about the steak he had eaten.

On the cruise to Leningrad from New York, John is a silent observer. They dress for dinner. John moves like a bear, and Mary, in her all-in-one girdle, minces her way across the deck, alighting by a railing to sip her consommé. Jane's teenage brothers wear suits. Her sister Ginny wears dresses with Peter Pan collars and curls her strawberry blonde hair to flirt with the elevator operator, traveling up and down all day. Jane wears scratchy Chubbettes shirtdresses. The Chubbettes ad in Life Magazine asks, "How happy can a chubby girl be?" The sky keeps its dusky light until almost midnight, and Jane pauses on the way to the ship's nightly smorgasbord to notice a couple on the deck, frenching.

"What are you looking at?" Hisses the girl, and then goes back to frenching. Jane skips off to the dining room, where she fills her plate with avocado halves. She has never before tasted an avocado, and on the cruise they fill the creamy fruit with blue cheese crumbles and drizzle it with vinaigrette. She has an avocado every day. After they have disembarked the ship, in the hotel in Leningrad, she dreams of them; in her dream, she reaches into her purse and finds that she has stolen avocados from the ship. They are covered with tiny pieces of candy and detritus that have collected in her purse's innards. Jane feels guilty, and ashamed, unsure of where to hide her stolen fruit. When she wakes up in the middle of the night, the light glows from behind the curtains.

The train station in Leningrad is filled with more workers than travelers. Every other person who passes holds a broom. The floor and ceilings are covered with mosaics; giant crystal chandeliers hang overhead. A man with a dark beard looks hard at Jane, then smiles to reveal the same silver-capped teeth as the girl who'd touched her coat. While boarding, Ginny spots a group of young soldiers. She winks at one of them, who winks back. Once in the stateroom, Ginny throws her bag on her bed and rummages through. She produces a tube of lipstick and applies it in the cramped bathroom, door open, leaning into the mirror to scowl at her pores.

Jane's brothers disappear immediately to find vodka. The stateroom is stuffy, shabby, but the furniture is dark, expensive-looking wood. The walls are paneled. Jane crouches on the bed, which creaks, like the train itself, and watches the window. The buildings, cheap high-rises, drip with nets to catch the pieces of their crumbling bricks. The businesses advertise in peeling signs, the letters all look like the symbol for pi.

"Let's go to the sitting car," suggests Ginny. "Do you want to wear some perfume?" She sprays Jane's wrist and they make their way to the sitting car, almost falling with each lurch of the train. They are covered with a thin veil of sweat when they arrive in the sitting car. It is filled with young soldiers in uniform, seventeen or eighteen, drunk and laughing. An empty bottle of vodka clanks against the metal radiator by their feet. A full bottle is being passed around. The soldier who winked at Ginny clears them both seats.

The soldier asks her something. "Da," Ginny says. They laugh. "Nyet," Ginny says, and they laugh more. "Hello madam," says a solider, nonsensically, to both of them.

They offer Ginny and Jane vodka, which they refuse. Jane is pressed against the muscular leg of a young man with dark hair and bright red circles on his cheeks. She asks him his name, and he laughs and shrugs: no English. Jane says, "I'm Jane," and he laughs again and takes the bottle of vodka. He offers it to her again – are you sure? – before taking an ambitious gulp. He chokes, chortles, and throws his head back; his neck is pale except for a birthmark, which reminds Jane of a crown.

In their own stateroom, John sits on the bed while Mary takes a sponge bath in the little lavatory. He is drinking a glass of rye whiskey, brought with him from Boston, no ice. He watches the landscape give way to suburbs, then countryside. The grass is long and occasionally dotted with roosters, draft horses, leaning fences, muddy ponds. The farm workers wear old-fashioned clothes, little Matryoshka dolls. He sips his whiskey and laments: even in another, strange country, there is nothing new to say.

Mary splashes her face and her mouth fills with water; she spits it out immediately, violently; she thinks, does it taste different? This Russian water? She considers, being careful not to ruin her perm with errant water drops. Maybe a little bit different. It wasn't colder, but it *tasted* colder.

When Ginny and Jane return to their stateroom, Ginny has forgotten about the elevator operator on the cruise. "What do you think his name is?" She asks Jane dreamily.

"Who?"

"The boy I was talking to, you drip!"

"Oh. I don't know."

There is a knock at the door. Ginny leaps up to answer it, disappointed to find a fat woman with a moustache standing with a cart.

"Samovar," says the woman, and entered the room. She

gives them cups of tea with sugar and milk, and trays of dark brown bread with butter and caviar. Jane eats hers on the bed, dusting crumbs from the front of her dress into the sheets. She licks the caviar off first, smashing it against the roof of her mouth, then eats a bite of bread, then a sip of tea. Close to dawn, her brothers enter the stateroom, having spent the whole bright night with the same soldiers Jane and Ginny had met in the sitting car, passing the bottle and shouting, sometimes in argument and sometimes to be heard over a fit of barking laughter. They spoke in English, the soldiers in Russian, nobody understanding a word that was said.

When they staggered off the train in Moscow – their balance destroyed by more than a week of alternating sea, land and rail – one of Jane's brothers vomits onto the tracks. A soldier exiting the train sees him and does the same. Ginny stares longingly through the window that leads to the sitting car, searching out her soldier whose name she does not know. Mary consults a notebook to find their hotel's address. John wonders how he will describe Moscow once they've returned, once he's back at work in Boston: but no, no, the walls, the train – everything is just the same, there is nothing new to say. The train coughs, the doors shut, and it disappears on a route to Beijing.

That night, at the Hotel Metropol, Jane dreams that she has stolen caviar from the fat woman on the train, clutching a big wet handful of eggs that smell like the sea; she is at school, raising her hand to answer a question.

"What's in your hand?" Her teacher asks. Jane is quiet. Her teacher comes to her desk and pries open her fist, revealing the small clot of black mush. The other students laugh, and when

Jane looks, they all have the face of the soldier she sat next to, and they are all wearing crowns.

FAILING, HE LIFTED WEIGHTS IN
THE THIRD COACH GYMNASIUM

AND HAD HIS MOUSTACHE TRIMMED
IN THE ADJOINING SALON —
JUST IN CASE SHE SHOULD APPEAR

HE DINED ALONE,
CRADLING HIS BORSCHT
ON A BEND NEAR OMSK,
FOLLOWED BY HASTY
PRAYERS IN THE
CHAPEL CAR

Four Thirty Five to Vladivostock
Will Hitchins

◼

It is 1984 and the long since forgotten Moscow based thrash metal band, Gulag and the Holidays, are boarding the four thirty five service to Vladivostok. The journey had been conceived of the previous afternoon by the group's erstwhile lead singer, Uncle Leni, and hurried travel arrangements were made. The reasons for the journey were muddled and confused, but essentially stemmed from the fact that the band were currently languishing in an artistic drought, neither Sasha Cumlovski's sadistically thrashed guitars, nor Uncle Leni's tonsillitis inducing screams were satisfying the politburo.

The release of the band's eponymous debut album, *As the (Iron) Curtain Falls*, had achieved the type of admiration within the Soviet Union normally reserved for bear baiters and cosmonauts. That was nine years ago, however, and the group's subsequent releases had fallen, if not on deaf ears, then certainly on waxy and ear plugged ones. Joseph Abelmann, the hopelessly idiosyncratic *Pravda* music critic wrote in one review:

> "How the mighty have fallen. There was once a time when, hidden within their down tuned E strings and double bass drum pedals this band provided us with a glimpse at our own mortality,

Dionysus and Apollo in eternal struggle, like an open wound, Uncle Leni's screams announced to us in a glorious thrash fanfare the ultimate tragedy of the human condition. Not today, however, not today. *Ring O Ring O Cadavers* is as bland as a bowl of street side borsch and leaves you feeling equally as nauseous".

The group were often criticised for their refusal to take a political standpoint of any kind whatsoever, particularly considering they were active in such a volatile period of history. In response to such challenges Leni would simply reply, "Metal music is above, beyond, and mutually exclusive to politics. Every note, quaver, semi quaver of Shostakovich's work suffered each and every time he criticised the party. Luckily we weren't invited to the party". This statement had little meaning and made even less sense but Uncle Leni felt it had a certain ring to it, like a cymbal tapped gently in a slate quarry, which incidentally was the totality of instrumentation of the hidden track on *As the (Iron) Curtain Falls*.

It had occurred to Leni that a brief sojourn into the heartland of Mother Russia, among the downtrodden miners and political dissidents, may act as a jump-start to a long overdue creative outpouring. He imagined himself and fellow band members, swimming in Lake Baikal covered in nothing but their bare tattooed skin and skull themed jewellery, coming up with new and revolutionary ways to play a down tuned power chord.

At the time, of course, such free travel across the Soviet

Union was strictly controlled. Tamara Luria, the daughter of the Minister for Culture, however, had been a huge fan of the group, and due to the questionable quality of their recent output, the Minister's home life was becoming increasingly difficult, Tamara taken as she was to insurmountable fits of rage. The result of this being that when the Minister was approached one afternoon by Gulag and the Holiday's manager, asking cautiously for permission for the group to travel overland to Siberia, he was more than willing, declaring it in the immediate and long lasting interest of the Proletariat that the band take this artistic sabbatical.

Due less to financial constraints and more to inane governmental regulations, the group were allocated a smaller cabin than they felt their status should have dictated, regardless, Levi was content to be moving away from Moscow, with its grey tower blocks and stayed musical vanguard, with their suffocating rules on how one *should* write a song about Death, or the Devil or self harm. For reasons that need not be explained, Uncle Levi had placed a veto on the bringing of instruments on the journey, however, Gori the Bassist (as he was then known) had managed inexplicably to smuggle a Theremin upon his person and was beginning to draw out the opening notes of November Rain, dancing with the invisible electrical current as a conductor on opening night. It was dusk by the time he had finished the final solo and collapsed exhausted on his bunk. This did not bode well for the rest of the journey.

It had in fact been some time since the group were in such close proximity. With only a thin walkway separating the two bunk beds, having a moment to themselves was next to impossible, and Saul the Drummer (as he is still known) would regularly wake in the middle of the night to make himself green tea on the portable stove. During the dizzying heights of the *Fall of the (Iron) Curtain* tour, when both svetlanas and babushkas alike were fighting in the aisles to lay with the most desired men on the Soviet arts scene, he had entered a whirlwind romance with the wife of the Chinese ambassador and the Green Tea habit he picked up at this time had never left him.

The train had just pulled away from Novosibirsk and it occurred to Uncle Leni that in two days travelling not one creative idea had emerged. He wasn't quite sure exactly what he meant by a creative idea, or what one entailed, but he knew that was what the outfit needed. He remembered reading an interview once with Z.Z. Top where he mentioned that ideas came to him 'organically'. Leni did not know the meaning of this word but as he looked out the window he rolled it around his mouth, feeling it out, trying it on for size.

Looking upon the snow stained wastelands flying by the window Uncle Leni felt a type of uneasy peace taking hold of him. It was ten minutes before he began to smell the methane and realised that Saul had left the small cabin cooker on, the fumes gently lulling him towards a final, irritatingly quiet end.

By the fourth day the four members of Gulag and the Holidays were barely speaking a word. Not out of any malice or bad blood, but out of boredom. The scenery rolled on without much significant change, and the only sound that could be heard was the gentle rumbling of the engine beneath the floorboards of their cabin. For a few hours they became an impromptu acapella outfit composing simple gospel spirituals underpinned by the clunkety-clunk of the train's wheels against the metal tracks. Gori the Theraminist (as he was by that point called) would sporadically holler out words which would be promptly answered by the others. These words ranged from the mundane to the obscene, finally ending with the four grown men shouting expletives at the top of their lungs out the window of the speeding train, before passing out for the following six hours.

The only food available on the restaurant car was poached herring with bellinis on the side, fine for one day, perhaps two, but a hard dish to stomach on four consecutive days. It was this frustration with the cuisine, perhaps, that was the proverbial backbreaking straw. On the fifth day, Uncle Leni stood up abruptly, knocking over the long since discarded Theremin as he did so, and declared to his companions that he was leaving the band, and would continue alone on the train to Mongolia. After which he intended to make his way south to Phnom Penh, and in the footsteps of one of his idols, take a holiday in Cambodia. Of course, the irony of this particular Dead Kennedy's song, and indeed their whole back catalogue was lost somewhere in translation. All he knew was that he looked good in black, and it was apparently the nation's dress code.

You have been reading

Galleons

Joshua Allen · fireland.com
Joshua Allen is a writer living in Denver, Colorado. The New York Times recently called him "rapaciously funny," which sounds sort of bad.

Always With Honor · alwayswithhonor.com
Always With Honor is the collective work of Elsa, Tyler and Zoe. Their mission is to create work that simplifies, synthesizes and clarifies. Zoe is a dog.

Paul Ford · ftrain.com
Paul Ford is a writer who lives in Brooklyn with his wife Mo. He is the author of the novel *Gary Benchley, Rock Star*.

Lizzy Stewart · abouttoday.co.uk
Lizzy Stewart is an illustrator based in Edinburgh. Her work is inspired primarily by a need to tell stories but also by folk culture, music and the city in which she lives.

Michael Crowe · michaelcrowe.org
Michael Crowe is inspired by Iris Murdoch, CF and Danny Ainge.

Luke Pearson · lukepearson.com

Luke Pearson is an illustrator and comics artist from the UK. He graduated in 2010 and is the creator of the comics *Hildafolk* and *Everything We Miss.*

Nikola Tesla

Matthew Allard · matthewallard.com

Matthew Allard is a fiction writer living in Los Angeles, California. He is the author of *To Slow Down the Time,* an illustrated story collection inspired by the artwork of Ian Dingman.

Meg Hunt · meghunt.com

Meg Hunt likes to draw pictures. One day she will go off into the sunset, singing songs and writing wrongs, but for now illustrating will do.

Daniel Beirne · thebitterend.tv

Daniel is a writer and actor living in Montreal.

Damien Correll · damiencorrell.com

Damien Correll is an art director and artist living and working in Brooklyn, NY where he is one half of the small design studio, Part & Parcel.

Meaghan O'Connell · meaghano.com

Meaghan O'Connell is a writer who lives in Brooklyn. She co-edited the nonfiction anthology *Coming & Crying.*

Richard Sanderson · rjsanderson.co.uk

Richard Sanderson is an illustrator who grew up on a farm in the Suffolk countryside. After several clumsy escape attempts he ended up in Bristol and studied illustration. He now lives and works from his studio in London.

The Trans-Siberian Railway
John Moe · twitter.com/johnmoe
John lives in St Paul where he hosts public radio shows and tends to kids. He writes for all sorts of places.

Gavin Potenza · gavinpotenza.com
Gavin Potenza is a designer in Brooklyn. He focuses his efforts on translating ideas into comprehensible visual solutions. He also co-runs the emerging design studio, Script & Seal.

Tess Lynch · tesslynch.tumblr.com
Tess Lynch is a writer and actor living in Los Angeles.

William Goldsmith · williamgoldsmith.co.uk
William Goldsmith is a Brighton-based illustrator. His first graphic novel *Vignettes of Ystov* was published by Jonathan Cape in March 2011.

Will Hitchins
Will Hitchins is an independent film-maker. Of sorts.

Josh Parpan · rparpan.blogspot.com
Josh Parpan works as a designer in the animation industry. His work has also appeared in print for the Image Comics anthology, *Popgun Vol. 3*.

Index